Jasmine
the Present
Fairy

To a very special Jasmine —
Miss Jasmine Grewal — with lots of love

Special thanks to
Narinder Dhami

ISBN 978-0-545-26694-9

12 11 10 9 8 7 6 5 4 3 2 1   10 11 12 13 14 15/0

Printed in the U.S.A.   40

First Scholastic Book Clubs printing, September 2010

Jasmine
the Present
Fairy

by Daisy Meadows

SCHOLASTIC INC.

New York   Toronto   London   Auckland
Sydney   Mexico City   New Delhi   Hong Kong

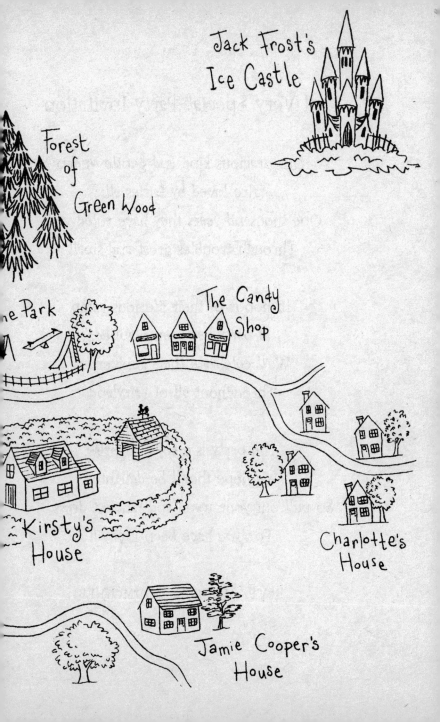

A Very Special Party Invitation

Our gracious king and gentle queen
Are loved by fairies all.
One thousand years they have ruled well,
Through troubles great and small.

In honor of their glorious reign
A party has been planned.
We'll celebrate their anniversary
Throughout all of Fairyland.

The party is a royal surprise,
We hope they'll be delighted.
So pull out your wand and fanciest dress . . .
For *you* have been invited!

RSVP: THE FAIRY GODMOTHER

Contents

A Special Street Party

"Look at all those booths, Rachel," Kirsty Tate said, pointing down the street where she lived. "This is going to be a great party!"

All of Kirsty's neighbors were rushing around, setting up booths and tables outside their houses. There were all kinds of things going on, from games and raffles to booths selling homemade jams and cakes. Delicious smells wafted toward the girls from the barbecue at the other end of the street. The road was closed to traffic, and people were already milling around in the sunshine, enjoying the fair.

"I think having a block party is a great idea," Rachel Walker, Kirsty's best friend, said with a grin. "I wish we had one on our street back home." Rachel had come to stay with Kirsty for the week of school break.

Kirsty was opening the last box of books. "We'd better hurry and put these on the table," she said. "Lots of people are showing up now."

"I'm glad the block party is today, since I'm going home tomorrow," Rachel said, helping Kirsty arrange the books around the booth that Mr. and Mrs. Tate were running. "I hope we raise lots of money for charity."

"We always do," said Kirsty happily, neatly stacking the books. "People come to the party from all over town. But"— she lowered her voice—"we'll have to be extra careful this year, won't we?"

Rachel nodded seriously. "Yes," she agreed. "A party means we have to keep our eyes out for goblin mischief!"

Rachel and Kirsty shared a wonderful secret. They had become friends with the fairies! Now, whenever their fairy friends were in trouble, Rachel and Kirsty were happy to help. The cause of the trouble was usually mean, prickly Jack Frost, who was always causing problems in Fairyland. This time, Jack Frost was determined to ruin the secret celebration that the Fairy Godmother and the seven Party Fairies were planning for the fairy king and queen's 1000th anniversary.

Jack Frost had sent his awful goblins into the human world to ruin as many parties as they could. Whenever the Party Fairies had flown to the rescue, the goblins tried to steal their magic party bags. They wanted to give the bags to Jack Frost, so he could use their special magic to throw a fabulous party of his own! But Rachel and Kirsty had managed to stop the goblins so far. They had helped six of the Party Fairies to keep their party bags safe.

"I'm not going to let Jack Frost's goblins ruin our block party," Kirsty said in a determined voice. "Or the king and queen's celebration!"

Rachel nodded in agreement as Kirsty's parents hurried toward them.

"You've done good job," Mrs. Tate smiled, admiring the neat piles of books.

"I think you two girls have worked hard enough," Mr. Tate added, as customers began to gather around the booth. "How about you go and explore the fair?"

"Great!" Kirsty whispered to Rachel, as they walked away. "Now we have a chance to look for goblins!"

The girls wandered happily through the crowd. There were lots of games, such as mini-bowling, hook-a-duck, and a special raffle called tombola, and there were tables piled with hand-sewn clothes,

toys, homemade pickles, and other things
for sale.

Rachel stopped at a bakery stand.
Her mouth watered as she looked at the
delicious display of tarts, cakes, and pies.
"Cherry the Cake Fairy would be proud
of those." She laughed.

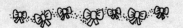

"There's no sign of any goblin trouble," said Kirsty. "Let's take a turn on the tombola."

The tombola was a big drum that spun around and gave out raffle numbers. Kirsty's neighbor, Mr. Cooper, was in charge of it, and there was already a line. Kirsty and Rachel stood behind a little girl and her mom.

The girl was staring up at the prizes on the shelves behind the tombola. "I hope I win a stuffed animal, Mommy," she said excitedly.

"Any ticket ending in four wins a prize!" called Mr. Cooper, spinning the tombola around.

Rachel and Kirsty watched as the little girl pulled out a purple ticket. She unfolded it carefully.

"Mommy, I won!" She gasped. "It's number 214."

"That's great!" her mom said with a laugh.

"Let's hope it's a stuffed animal," Rachel whispered to Kirsty, as the little girl handed Mr. Cooper the ticket.

But Kirsty had already spotted the prize with purple ticket 214 pinned to it. "It's not," she said, pointing. "Look."

The prize was a blue, plastic apron with a picture of a fluffy, white kitten on the front. Kirsty hoped the little girl wouldn't be too disappointed.

"Okay, let me find your prize," said Mr. Cooper, scanning the shelves. "It's here somewhere. . . ."

But just before he spotted the apron, something magical happened. Rachel and Kirsty saw a shower of blue sparkles appear out of thin air and whirl around the apron. The next moment, the apron had vanished. In its place sat a fluffy, white toy kitten, with a blue satin bow around its neck! Pinned to the bow was purple ticket 214.

"I won the white kitten!" the little girl cried joyfully.

Looking puzzled, Mr. Cooper lifted the toy down. "I don't remember seeing that prize before," he muttered.

Kirsty and Rachel grinned at each other as Mr. Cooper handed the

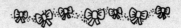

kitten to the delighted little girl.

"That was fairy magic," whispered Kirsty.

Rachel nodded. "And that means there must be a Party Fairy very close by!"

Unlucky Draw!

The little girl skipped off happily, clutching her prize. Kirsty and Rachel snuck behind the tombola booth to look for the fairy. They couldn't see any sign of her.

"Rachel! Kirsty!" The girls suddenly heard a voice calling from above their heads. "I'm up here!"

The girls looked up at a string of colored flags tied to the top of the booth, and there was Jasmine the Present Fairy. She was balancing on the string like an acrobat on a tightrope!

"Hello," Kirsty and Rachel called, smiling up at her.

Jasmine fluttered down to join them, her straight brown hair flying out behind her. She wore a long, blue skirt with a ruffled hemline that swirled around her ankles, and a cropped top in the same shade of blue. On her feet were dark blue ballet shoes with satin ribbons. She carried a glittering blue wand in her hand.

"I'm here to make sure that your block party goes well," she explained, "and that all the prizes are as perfect as possible." She smiled at Rachel and Kirsty. "And that means making sure no goblins try to ruin the party!" she added in a determined voice.

"Have you seen any goblins?" Rachel asked anxiously.

"No—" Jasmine began, but she was interrupted by the sound of someone crying loudly. It came from the booth next to the tombola.

"Someone sounds upset," Kirsty whispered. "Maybe we'd better take a look." Jasmine flew down and hid on Rachel's shoulder, behind her hair. Then they hurried over to join the line at a booth called "Luck of the Draw." A little boy was standing by a big barrel of sawdust, crying bitterly. He had a toy plane in his hand.

Kirsty knew how the game worked.

Each kid got a chance to search for a prize in the giant barrel of sawdust.

"I loved the plane when I unwrapped it," the boy wailed. "But look, Dad, the wings are broken!"

"This could be goblin trouble," Jasmine whispered in Rachel's ear.

"I'm very sorry," said the man at the Luck of the Draw booth. "I tell you what, why don't you pull out another prize for free?"

The boy stopped crying immediately.
"Thank you!" He smiled.

Rachel, Kirsty, and Jasmine watched as the little boy put his hand into the sawdust bin and pulled out a small package. He unwrapped it eagerly, but they all stared in horror when a moldy old apple fell out!

"Oh, no!" Jasmine gasped.

The little boy began to cry again.

Meanwhile, the man behind the booth was looking very flustered. "I think somebody's playing an awful joke on me!" he said. "Don't cry." He patted the little boy on the shoulder. "Have another try."

The three friends watched anxiously as the boy pulled out his third wrapped prize. This time, he unwrapped a toy car without any wheels!

"All the presents in the prize bin are horrible," Kirsty whispered to Rachel and Jasmine. "What are we going to do?"

The little boy was about to burst into tears again, but the kind man running the booth saved the day.

"Look," he said, leaning across to the stall next door, which he was also running. "I'll give you one of these prizes, instead." He handed the boy a shiny bat and ball set.

"Great!" the boy said happily, showing it to his dad as they walked away.

"This is definitely goblin trouble!" Jasmine said as the man bent over the sawdust barrel and began looking through it. "But I'll fix everything with my party magic."

"That's exactly what the goblin's hoping for," Kirsty whispered, looking worried. "Don't take out your party bag—he's just waiting for a chance to steal it!"

"I can't worry about that," Jasmine whispered, glancing at the boys and girls behind them. "The children will be so disappointed if I don't fix the Luck of the Draw game."

"Well, we'll help," Rachel said. "Kirsty, let's make sure the booth owner doesn't notice Jasmine. And keep your eyes peeled for goblins."

The man was looking very concerned. "I don't think you should take a turn, girls," he said. "I may have to close my games."

"No, don't do that,"

Rachel said quickly. "I'd like to try your hook-a-duck game. What are the rules?"

While the man was talking to Rachel, Jasmine slid quietly off her shoulder and flew down to the sawdust tub. Meanwhile, Kirsty stood right in front of the tub so that nobody in the line could see what was happening. She was watching for goblins, too.

Quickly, Jasmine opened her party bag and took out a handful of sparkling blue fairy dust, shaped like tiny bows. She sprinkled it over the barrel and gave a

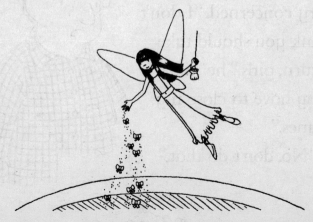

sigh of relief. "All done!" she whispered to Kirsty.

But just then, there was an awful noise from *inside* the sawdust tub. Suddenly, a green goblin popped up and grabbed at Jasmine's party bag!

Girls on the Run

"Oh!" Jasmine and Kirsty both gasped as the goblin lunged toward them.

Luckily, Jasmine was too quick for him. She whisked the party bag out of his reach. Muttering angrily, the goblin leaped out of the tub and darted out of sight behind the booth.

Still shaking with fright, Jasmine
fluttered up to sit on Kirsty's
shoulder. But as she landed,
her party bag slipped
from her trembling
fingers. It fell straight
into the Luck of the
Draw tub and
disappeared in the sawdust.

"Oh, no!" Kirsty groaned.

Over the shoulder of the booth owner,
Rachel had seen what was happening.
Somehow they had to get Jasmine's
party bag back — and fast. "Um, actually
I don't want to play hook-a-duck," she
said quickly. "I think I'll try Luck of the
Draw instead."

The man looked amazed. "Are you

sure?" he asked. "It doesn't seem very lucky at the moment."

"I'm positive," Rachel said firmly.

"Me, too," Kirsty added, guessing what Rachel was up to.

The two girls handed over their money. Kirsty went first and Rachel, Jasmine, and the booth owner watched as she felt around inside the tub. Her fingers closed around something and she pulled it out. But it was one of the wrapped presents, not Jasmine's party bag. Inside the package was a beautiful blue mini-kite.

"At least the presents are OK now," Jasmine whispered in Kirsty's ear.

"Your turn," said the booth owner, looking at Rachel. But just then, one of the children at the hook-a-duck game gave a cry of alarm. He had accidentally caught his fishing rod on the string of flags! 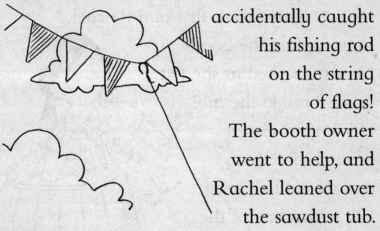 The booth owner went to help, and Rachel leaned over the sawdust tub. But just as Rachel was taking her turn, Kirsty gasped.

"Watch out!" she whispered. "The goblin is climbing up the leg of the table!"

Sure enough, the goblin was clambering up the leg of the table back toward the sawdust tub, with a very determined look on his face.

"You're the only one with a turn left, Rachel," Kirsty whispered anxiously. "You have to get Jasmine's party bag before the goblin does!"

Quickly, Rachel plunged her hand into the sawdust and began to feel around. She wondered how she would know when she'd found the party bag. Just then, she felt something tingle under her fingers. "Fairy magic!" Rachel said to herself, and she pulled out the object.

Both girls gasped with relief—it was Jasmine's party bag!

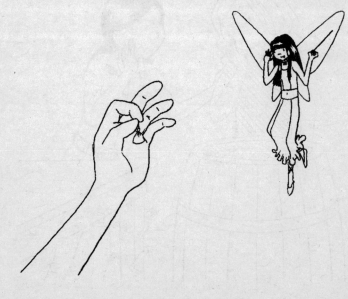

"Hooray!" Jasmine cried happily. "Thanks, Rachel."

At that moment, the goblin peeked over the edge of the tub. He grinned when he saw the party bag, and made another grab for it. Rachel managed to jump away from him, clutching the bag tightly.

"Let's get out of here," Kirsty suggested. "Quick, back to my house!"

The girls and Jasmine darted behind the booth and ran away from the fair toward the Tates' house. But the goblin chased after them.

Rachel glanced over her shoulder. "He's not far behind!" she panted.

They reached the house, and Kirsty let them in through the front door. But the goblin was charging toward them, and the girls barely managed to slam the door shut in time. "We have to get rid of that goblin," Jasmine said urgently.

"I've got an idea!" Kirsty declared
suddenly. "Rachel, you guard the door.
Jasmine, follow me."

Rachel nodded and waited
by the front door as Jasmine
and Kirsty rushed
into the living room.

Then a tiny sound
made Rachel jump.

Her heart thumping,
Rachel looked around. She
smiled to see Pearl, Kirsty's black-and-
white kitten, sitting at the top of the
stairs, watching her.

But then Rachel heard something else. It was the sound of the cat flap in the kitchen door creaking open. Rachel frowned. If Pearl was sitting on the stairs, then who was coming in?

She crept along the hall toward the kitchen and gasped at what she saw. The goblin was climbing in through the cat flap!

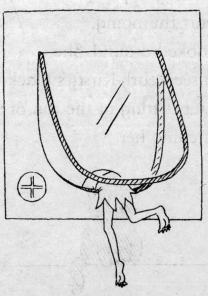

Rachel turned toward the living room in a panic.

"Kirsty! Jasmine!" she shouted. "Look out—the goblin's coming!"

Would her warning be enough?

All Wrapped Up

In the living room, Jasmine looked at Kirsty with alarm. "What should we do?" she cried.

But Kirsty was picking up an empty cardboard box that had been full of books for the booth. "If we can make the goblin believe your party bag is in this box, we might be able to trap him inside!" she said.

"Can you make a trail of magic sparkles leading into the box?"

"I can do better than that!" Jasmine replied eagerly. She opened her party bag and sprinkled some glittering fairy dust onto the cardboard. Immediately, it changed into a beautiful blue gift box, with a lovely gold ribbon lying beside it. Then Jasmine sprinkled a trail of fairy dust into the box, and she and Kirsty hurried out of sight behind the couch.

No sooner were Kirsty and Jasmine hidden than the goblin dashed into the living room and skidded to a halt, closely followed by Rachel.

Poor Rachel couldn't believe her eyes when she saw the trail of fairy dust and no sign of Kirsty and Jasmine. "Oh, no!" she said quietly. "If the party bag is in the box, the goblin can take it!"

The goblin had also spotted the fairy dust trail, and he was grinning. "Ha!" he chuckled gleefully, sticking his tongue out at Rachel. "Jack Frost is going to be so happy with me when

41

I give him a magic party bag!" Still
chuckling, he crawled into the box.

Immediately, Jasmine and Kirsty rushed
out from behind the
couch. Rachel, who
wasn't expecting
it, jumped with
surprise.
"Quick, Rachel!"
cried Kirsty. "Help
me close the box!"
Rachel jumped

forward, and she and Kirsty shut the lid.

Then Jasmine waved her wand, and
the gold ribbon floated up into the air
and tied itself firmly around the box.
There was a cry of rage from inside as the
goblin realized he'd been tricked.

"So that's what you were up to!" Rachel laughed.

"Let me out!" the goblin roared.

"I don't think so," Kirsty replied.

"Should we send the goblin back to Jack Frost by magic fairy mail?" Jasmine suggested.

The girls nodded and Jasmine waved her wand again. There was a shower of fairy dust and a label appeared on the box. It said JACK FROST, ICE CASTLE in big letters. Then, in another swirl of glittering magic, the package vanished completely.

Fairyland Fun

Kirsty turned to Rachel. "We did it!" she declared. "We saved all the Party Fairies' magic party bags!"

"That means the anniversary party for our king and queen can go on without any more trouble from Jack Frost," Jasmine announced happily. "And it's all thanks to you two."

Kirsty and Rachel grinned proudly at each other.

Then Kirsty spotted something. "Look!" she cried, pointing at the window.

A rainbow of shimmering colors streamed through the glass. The girls blinked in wonder as one end of the beautiful rainbow came to rest on the floor beside them.

"It's the magic rainbow to take us to Fairyland!" Rachel breathed.

"Remember, Kirsty? Bertram said
the Fairy Godmother would send a
rainbow for us when it was time for the
anniversary party."

"Oh!" Kirsty cried. "But we're not
ready! We don't have our party
clothes on."

Jasmine laughed.
"Just step onto
the end of the
rainbow, girls," she
told them. "We
Party Fairies will
help you get ready
when you arrive
in Fairyland." She
waved her wand.

"See you very soon!" she called, as she
vanished in a swirl of glitter.

"Come on, Kirsty," Rachel said, taking her friend's hand.

Together, the girls stepped carefully onto the rainbow. Immediately, there was a whooshing sound. They were surrounded by golden fairy dust as the rainbow whisked them away.

"Here they are!" called a joyful voice.

As the golden sparkles cleared, the girls found themselves in the Great Hall of the Party Workshop in Fairyland. They were already fairy-size themselves, with glittering wings on their backs. And they could see Jasmine and the six other Party Fairies smiling at them!

"Welcome to the party!" they cried.

"Wow!" Rachel exclaimed, looking around.

Last time the girls had been there, the Party Fairies had been busy with preparations. Now everything was ready. All the fairies were there to welcome the king and queen, and they were dressed in their best party outfits. Grace the Glitter Fairy had been busy decorating the hall with sparkling streamers,

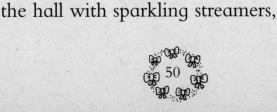

rainbow balloons, and jeweled
lanterns. There were also
tiny, white twinkling lights
strung all over the ceiling.
Rachel and Kirsty had
never seen anything
so beautiful!
In one corner, the
frog orchestra was
playing a
cheerful tune.
In another, presents
were piled up,
all beautifully
wrapped by Jasmine and
tied with satin bows
in rainbow colors. There
were bowls of candy placed here
and there. On a golden table stood a

huge cake shaped like the king and queen's palace.

Rachel and Kirsty were amused to see the goblin who had tried to steal Cherry the Cake Fairy's party bag, fussing over the cake.

"Now don't touch the icing," he was telling the fairies standing around the table. "I spent ages making sure it looked exactly like the palace!"

"He seems to be enjoying himself," Rachel whispered to Kirsty.

"I'm so happy to see you, girls," the Fairy Godmother declared as she hurried toward them. Her green eyes twinkled with happiness, and the jewels on her golden dress sparkled in the candlelight. "We're so grateful that you made sure our party wasn't ruined by Jack Frost!" She turned to Phoebe the Fashion Fairy. "I think Phoebe has something for you."

"I do!" Phoebe laughed. "How about some beautiful new dresses for the party, girls?"

"Oh, yes please!" Kirsty and Rachel cried together.

Phoebe smiled and threw a handful of sparkling fairy dust over them. Both girls closed their eyes.

Kirsty was the first to open them again. "Oh, Rachel!" she gasped. "These are the most beautiful dresses I've ever seen!"

Rachel opened her eyes to see Kirsty wearing a long, sparkling rose-pink-and-gold dress, with pink ballet shoes and a glittering pink tiara. Rachel wore the same, but her outfit was in shimmering purple and silver. "Thank you, Phoebe—" the girls began.

But before they could say any more, a little fairy zoomed into the Great Hall, panting with excitement. "The king and queen are here!" she cried.

Party Time!

Everyone began to talk at once, but the
Fairy Godmother raised her wand for
silence. "Now remember," she called,
"when the king and queen get out
of their carriage, everybody shouts,
'SURPRISE!'"

Rachel, Kirsty, and all the fairies
crowded around the door.

A shining crystal carriage, pulled by six white unicorns and driven by Bertram, the frog footman, was making its way toward them. The carriage stopped and Bertram hopped down to open the door. Out stepped the fairy king and queen.

"SURPRISE!" everybody shouted— Rachel and Kirsty loudest of all!

The king and queen looked confused

for a moment, but then they saw the golden banner that hung over the castle door: CONGRATULATIONS TO OUR BELOVED KING OBERON AND QUEEN TITANIA ON THEIR 1000TH ANNIVERSARY!

"Oh!" the queen exclaimed, looking delighted. "How wonderful!"

"I think our Party Fairies have had a hand in this," the king said joyfully.

The Fairy Godmother stepped forward. "Welcome, King Oberon and Queen Titania!" she announced. "But the Party Fairies aren't the only ones who have helped to make this party special. We must also thank our friends, Rachel and Kirsty." She turned to smile at the girls. "Once again, they have saved us from Jack Frost's mischief."

"Thank you, girls," said the king warmly. "You must tell us the whole story later."

"You both look beautiful," the queen added with a smile. "Now, let's forget all about Jack Frost, and enjoy the party!"

Rachel and Kirsty had never been
to a party like this before
in their lives. The frog
orchestra played
catchy tunes, specially
created by Melodie
the Music Fairy, and
all the fairies danced
and fluttered around
like colorful butterflies.

Then there were party
games, organized by Polly the
Party Fun Fairy: Pass the Magic Present,
Musical Magical Chairs, and many more.

The treats made by Honey the Candy
Fairy were so delicious that Rachel
and Kirsty just couldn't
stop eating the
Strawberry Sparkles.

After the games,
everyone gathered
around to watch the king and queen open
their presents and then cut the wonderful
cake, made by Cherry and iced by the
goblin. All too soon, the party was over.

"I hope you had a good time, girls,"
Queen Titania said, smiling at Rachel
and Kirsty.

"It was great!" Rachel declared.

"The best party ever!" Kirsty added.

"It's time for you to go home now," the
queen went on. She waved her wand, and
a shimmering rainbow appeared beside
them. "But before you go, I think the
Party Fairies have something for you."

Jasmine and Cherry
flew forward.

"These are from
all of us!" Jasmine said,
handing Kirsty a pink,
sparkly party bag,
while Cherry gave Rachel
a purple one. "Don't look in
them until you get home."

"Thank you," Kirsty and Rachel replied, waving at their friends. "See you again soon, we hope."

"Good-bye!" answered all the fairies.

And with the voices of their fairy friends ringing in their ears, the girls stepped onto the rainbow. Moments later, they found themselves in the Tates' kitchen, back to their usual size and wearing their normal clothes once again.

"Oh, that was magical!" Kirsty sighed happily.

Rachel was already opening her party bag. "Look, Kirsty!" she exclaimed in delight.

The bags were full of presents from their Party Fairy friends. There was a piece of annivesary cake from Cherry, a fairy music CD from Melodie, a tub of glittery lip gloss from Grace, a silk bag of candy from Honey, a pack of magic playing cards from Polly, and a sparkly bracelet from Phoebe. And Jasmine had given them each a golden jewelry box with a revolving fairy on top to put all their presents in.

Rachel and Kirsty couldn't believe their eyes!

"We must be the luckiest girls in the world," Rachel sighed.

"And we can still enjoy the rest of the block party, too," Kirsty added.

Later that night, the girls lay in their beds in Kirsty's room, still too excited to sleep. The jewelry boxes, filled with presents, sat on the dresser.

"It's sad that I have to go home tomorrow," Rachel said with a yawn. "But I've really enjoyed our latest fairy adventure, and I know we'll see each other again soon."

"Me, too," Kirsty agreed, starting to feel sleepy at last. She closed her eyes.

There was silence for a few moments. Then, "I can hear something," Rachel said. "It's coming from our jewelry boxes!"

The soft, tinkling sound of party music filled the room.

"Fairy magic!" Kirsty said happily, snuggling down under her comforter. "Good night, Rachel."

Come flutter by Butterfly Meadow

#1: Dazzle's First Day

#2: Twinkle Dives In

#3: Three Cheers for Mallow!

#4: Skipper to the Rescue

#5: Dazzle's New Friend

#6: Twinkle and the Busy Bee

#7: Joy's Close Call

#8: Zippy's Tall Tale

#9: Skipper Gets Spooked

RAINBOW magic™

There's Magic in Every Series!

The Rainbow Fairies

The Weather Fairies

The Jewel Fairies

The Pet Fairies

The Fun Day Fairies

The Petal Fairies

The Dance Fairies

The Music Fairies

The Sports Fairies

The Party Fairies

Read them all!

📖 SCHOLASTIC

HIT entertainment

www.scholastic.com

www.rainbowmagiconline.com

RMFAIRY2

RAINBOW magic™

SPECIAL EDITION

Three Books in One— More Rainbow Magic Fun!

■SCHOLASTIC
www.scholastic.com
www.rainbowmagiconline.com

HIT entertain

RMSPEC

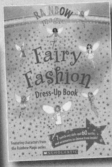

Perfectly Princess

Don't miss these royal adventures!

Printed on colored pages!